D1412262

First published in Great Britain in 2001 by Brimax
an imprint of Octopus Publishing Group Ltd
2-4 Heron Quays, London E14 4JP
© Octopus Publishing Group Ltd

ISBN 1 85854 170 0
Printed in China

Rainbow Fairies

Eric Kincaid

ONE DAY IN THE COUNTRYSIDE when the thunder and lightning had stopped, a beautiful arch appeared in the blue sky. It was an arch of red, orange, yellow, green, blue, indigo and violet.

It was called a **rainbow**. This was the time when the Rainbow Fairies arrived.

It was always very exciting when the new Rainbow Fairies arrived, and all the older Rainbow Fairies gathered at the end of the rainbow to greet them.

As soon as the rainbow appeared in the sky, the baby Rainbow Fairies started to *slide* down the arch. Rainbow Fairies didn't come very often, but when they did there were lots and lots of them.

Unlike other types of fairy, the Rainbow Fairies arrived with wings already beautiful, for as they slid down the rainbow it brushed against them, painting them in all its lovely shades.

They bounced onto the grass and their wings *sparkled* as they tried flapping them for the very first time.

But there was one baby fairy who could not flap because one of her delicate little wings was torn.

The older fairies gathered around and tried to comfort her, but the poor little fairy was much too upset!

Queen Rainbow flew over and gently took the fairy by the hand. "Don't cry little one, we'll soon have that wing mended, and then you can fly with the other fairies."

"But how will you mend something so fine?" sobbed the baby fairy.

"We shall take you to a master who spins only the finest silk," replied the queen.

Queen Rainbow led the fairies through the grass to the bush where Old Spinny had his web and workshop.

When they arrived the fairies made a circle around the bush. Then Queen Rainbow went up to the cobweb, and *gently* touched it with her magical wand.

It was just enough to bring out the largest, friendliest spider you have ever seen. The spider crawled onto a large stone and looked up at Queen Rainbow.

"Hello, Old Spinny," she said, stroking his head.

"Would you be so kind as to mend this baby's wing? I think she was too excited and came down the rainbow much too fast."

"Well, well," said Old Spinny.
"Turn around and let me see what you have
done." He put on a large pair of spectacles
to see more clearly...

"Yes, I see the trouble, that little tear
won't take long to fix."

And he winked at the baby, who
smiled back shyly.

Old Spinny carefully tucked a thread of
finest gossamer into the torn wing. Then he
started to turn around as the silk came out
of the cobweb sac at the back of his body.

He turned delicately one way, and
then another, until the tear was completely
mended.

All this time the fairies had stood
watching in *wonder* as the baby fairy's
wing was made as good as new. Then the
fairies cheered loudly as the baby flew up
and down in delight.

Old Spinny gave what was left of his fine thread to the birds for their nests, and the fairies said goodbye to the kind and friendly spider.

Darkness was starting to fall over the fairy dell, and normally this is the time the baby fairies would go to bed. But not tonight, for a rainbow day is a special day, and tonight was just right for a party.

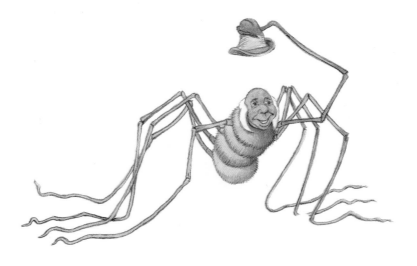